Aurora Presents
Don Bluth Productions'
The Secret of NIMH

Mrs. Brisby's
Remembering Game

Story Adapted by E.K. Davis • Illustrated by Jean Chandler

Golden Press • New York
Western Publishing Company, Inc., Racine, Wisconsin

Copyright © 1982 Mrs. Brisby Ltd. All rights reserved. Printed in the U.S.A. by Western Publishing Company, Inc.
No part of this book may be reproduced or copied in any form without written permission from the publisher.
GOLDEN®, A LITTLE GOLDEN SNIFF IT BOOK, and GOLDEN PRESS® are trademarks of Western Publishing Company, Inc. The "Microfragrance"™ labels were supplied by 3M Company. Library of Congress Catalog Card Number: 81-86489 ISBN 0-307-13209-9/ISBN 0-307-63209-1 (lib. bdg.)   A B C D E F G H I J

Illustrations are based on the original art from Don Bluth Productions' film THE SECRET OF NIMH.

The film THE SECRET OF NIMH is based upon the book MRS. FRISBY AND THE RATS OF NIMH by Robert C. O'Brien.

The Brisby house on Fitzgibbon farm was covered with deep drifts of snow.

"Why can't we go out, Mommy?" asked little Cynthia Brisby for the sixth time.

"Cynthia, there's too much snow," Mrs. Brisby said. "I know you're tired of being inside. We've played every game we can think of…except…I know! Let's play *Remember*! It's a great game. I choose summer when there's no snow at all and I'll go first."

"Hurray! *Remember*!" cheered the Brisby children.

Mrs. Brisby closed her eyes. "I'm remembering my favorite resting place," she said dreamily, "and how the sun makes me sleepy and how rich the raspberries smell. Now,

'Remember, remember. Yes, I do.
Next it's your turn, now it's you...Teresa!'"

"I remember gathering dandelions in the big green field outside our house and bringing them home for dandelion soup," Teresa said. "Now,
    'Remember, remember. Yes, I do.
    Next it's your turn, now it's you...Timmy!'"

Timmy remembered the old mill. "The water wheel
creaks and squeaks as it turns around. I lie on the moss
and smell the honeysuckle and watch."

Timmy chose his big brother Martin to go next.

"I remember the barn," said Martin. "I swing from the
rafters and slide down the hay...

...and climb up on the tractor. I like that oily smell."

Little Cynthia was last. She said, "I 'member when Mommy and I got the seeds."

"Yes, my baby," said Mrs. Brisby. "We got the sunflower seeds and brought them home so we could eat them in the winter time."

Suddenly there was a *clump*! from outside the house.
The door burst open and a bundled figure hurried in.

"Auntie Shrew!" everyone cried.

"Little as I like this dreadful weather," Auntie Shrew
said, "I have brought you a surprise."

Auntie Shrew unwrapped the surprise. It was a pan filled with golden brown cake.

"I was remembering summer and the grape arbor. Then I took some raisins, which are dried grapes, and I baked Auntie Shrew's Raisin Pan Cake."

"It's like magic!" Mrs. Brisby cried. "A summer treat on a winter's day!"